THE CAT IN THE

RHINESTONE SUIT

by **John Carter Cash** ★ illustrated by **Scott Nash**

Little Simon Inspirations

New York London Toronto Sydney New Delhi

THE CAT
in the rhinestone suit
has spurs on his
cowboy boots.

I would like to dedicate this book to my son Jack Ezra Cash. His inexhaustible energy and spirit forever reminds me that life is supposed to be fun.

—JCC. October, 2011.

For Caitlyn and Sean

—S.N.

LITTLE SIMON INSPIRATIONS

An imprint of Simon & Schuster Children's Publishing Division

1230 Avenue of the Americas, New York, New York 10020

Text copyright © 2012 by John Carter Cash. Illustrations copyright © 2012 by Scott Nash.

LITTLE SIMON INSPIRATIONS and associated colophon are trademarks of Simon & Schuster, Inc.

For information about special discounts for bulk purchases, please contact

Simon & Schuster Special Sales at 1-866-506-1949 or business@simonandschuster.com.

The Simon & Schuster Speakers Bureau can bring authors to your live event.

For more information or to book an event contact the Simon & Schuster Speakers Bureau

at 1-866-248-3049 or visit our website at www.simonspeakers.com.

Designed by Leyah Jensen and Giuseppe Castellano

Manufactured in China 0212 SCP

First Edition 10 9 8 7 6 5 4 3 2 1

ISBN 978-1-4169-7483-3

He rides on a
bandicoot
through the desert
all day.

THE MOUSE
in the wide-brimmed hat on Camel, behind the Cat, is off to Waterhole Flat

where the rattlesnakes play.

THE SNAKES
never bite or fight,
but they hiss and dance
all night,

then hide in the rocks
from sight
when the chilly winds blow.
Well . . .

who he'd
deemed bad
to the CORE
with no
goodness
to show.

When Cat was young and quite **small**,

the Snake swiped his catnip **ball**

and left him no toy at **all**,

so the Cat sat and he **cried**.

Mother Cat took silver **twine**
that glittered, sparkled,
and **shined**,
and sewed in
rhinestones so **fine**
till the Cat
glowed with **pride.**

**Now Cat keeps
a shiny star**
fastened
right above
his **heart.**
**He's now
vowed to do
his part**
to bring justice
to **bear.**
Now . . .

The day was so hot and long

that Cat hummed a lonesome song;
the 'Coot and the Mouse sang 'long—
without worry or care.

Then . . .

BANDICOOT

fell o'er a **stump,**

and he and the Cat— they **jumped.**

Camel
slammed
into them—
thump!

Then they
flew in
the air!

The Cat tumbled tail 'bove nose, and rhinestones flew off his clothes.

Where did they fly?
Well, who knows?

Oh dear, what dire despair!

CAT grabbed ahold of a **root**, and Camel clamped down on 'Coot,

who held
to Mouse
by the
boot
till they
hung
in
dire
sway.

They hung as eagles flew **high**,

too busy,
up in the **sky**.

A turtle crept by so **slow,** ears shut to pleas from **below.**

Straight on his way he did go, though they called and they **yelped.**

Would it be crazy to say they'd still be hanging **today**

had **Del Moore** not passed their **way** and offered them some **help?**

Del Moore lowered down his **tail** for Cat and his friends to **scale.**

They climbed right up to the **trail** where they fell in a **pile.** And . . .

Snake offered Cat his tail **end**.
Out the Cat's paw did **extend**.

Del Moore said,
"Let's just be **friends!**"
And the Cat gave a **smile**.

Now Cat and Mouse and ole Snake all live in a house by the lake. They pile up rhinestones with rakes that sparkle and glow.

Camel and 'Coot love to **dance**.
Join them if you get a **chance**.
Away with your cans and **can'ts**.
Become part of the **show**!

Trouble? Well, there's none at **all**.
The Snake gave Cat back his **ball**.
Greatest of pals after **all**,
they are seldom **apart**.